A Fish Named

GLUB

For Bruce, Laurie, Tom & Steve, Lenny, Louis & Joni.
None of whom I've met, but a fish can still dream. — D.B.

To my three little chicks — J.B.

Text © 2014 Dan Bar-el
Illustrations © 2014 Josée Bisaillon

Kids Can Press acknowledges the financial support of the Government of Ontario, through the Ontario Media Development Corporation's Ontario Book Initiative; the Ontario Arts Council; the Canada Council for the Arts; and the Government of Canada, through the CBF, for our publishing activity.

Published in Canada by
Kids Can Press Ltd.
25 Dockside Drive
Toronto, ON M5A 0B5

Published in the U.S. by
Kids Can Press Ltd.
2250 Military Road
Tonawanda, NY 14150

www.kidscanpress.com

The artwork in this book was rendered in mixed media.
The text is set in Warnock Pro, Romp and Luella.

Acquired by Tara Walker
Edited by Yvette Ghione
Designed by Karen Powers

This book is smyth sewn casebound.
Manufactured in Shenzhen, China, in 10/2013
through Asia Pacific Offset.

CM 14 0 9 8 7 6 5 4 3 2 1

Library and Archives Canada Cataloguing in Publication

Bar-el, Dan, author
      A fish named Glub / written by Dan Bar-el ;
illustrated by Josée Bisaillon.

ISBN 978-1-55453-812-6 (bound)

      I. Bisaillon, Josée, 1982–, illustrator II. Title.

PS8553.A76229F57 2014   jC813'.54   C2013-905549-5

Kids Can Press is a **corus**™ Entertainment company

A Fish Named
GLUB

Written by
DAN BAR-EL

Illustrated by
JOSÉE BISAILLON

KIDS CAN PRESS

Fish.

Fish in bowl.

"Who am I?" wonders fish.

"Glub!" A girl shouts, face pressed to glass. "Glub, glub!"

"Evelyn, come finish your biscuit," says her mom, Jenny. "Leave that poor fish alone."

"Oh," thinks fish. "I am Glub, all alone."

Glub in bowl. All alone.

"Where do I come from?" wonders Glub.

"Foster G. Willikers!" shouts an angry lady. "Where on earth did that fish come from?"

"Don't holler, Sis," sighs Foster, at the grill. "It came from the big guy upstairs. Whatsisname in apartment 2B. He must have made tracks past midnight. He left the fish."

"Honestly," huffs Sis, "I can't leave you alone for a minute."

"Oh," thinks Glub. "I come from the big guy upstairs. Whatsisname."

Glub in bowl, all alone. Far from home.

"What do I need?" wonders Glub.

"Hey, Foster, your fish needs fish food,"
says Pete. "Otherwise, he'll keel over."

"And clean water," says Doug.
"Otherwise, he's a goner."

"And better light," says Bernice.
"Otherwise, he'll scare himself
into the grave."

"Alright, alright," moans Foster.

"Alright, alright," worries Glub.

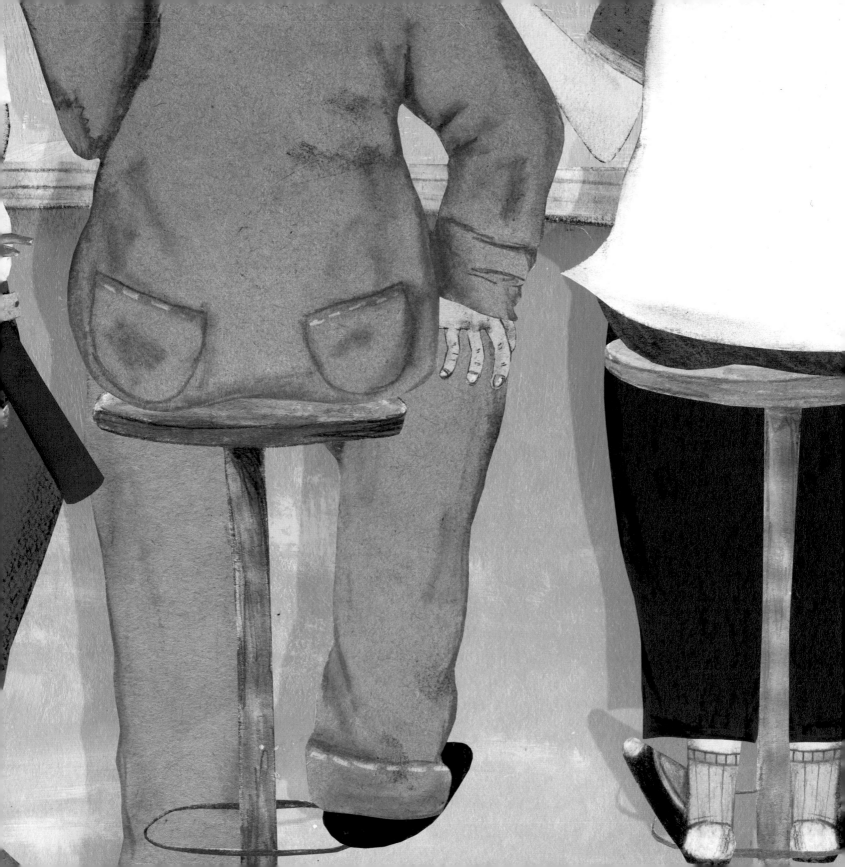

Glub in bowl, all alone, far from home.
Well-fed and, *phew*, still not dead.

"What *is* a home?" wonders Glub.

"Hi, Foster," says Jenny, ducking in at two
minutes to five. "Still time to get a piece
of pie in this joint?"

"For my two favorite customers? Anytime,
Jenny!" says Foster, putting down the mop.

"Hear that, Evelyn? Foster thinks we're special!"

Foster blushes red as a sundae cherry.

"Ah," thinks Glub, all tingly.

"Home is where the heart lives."

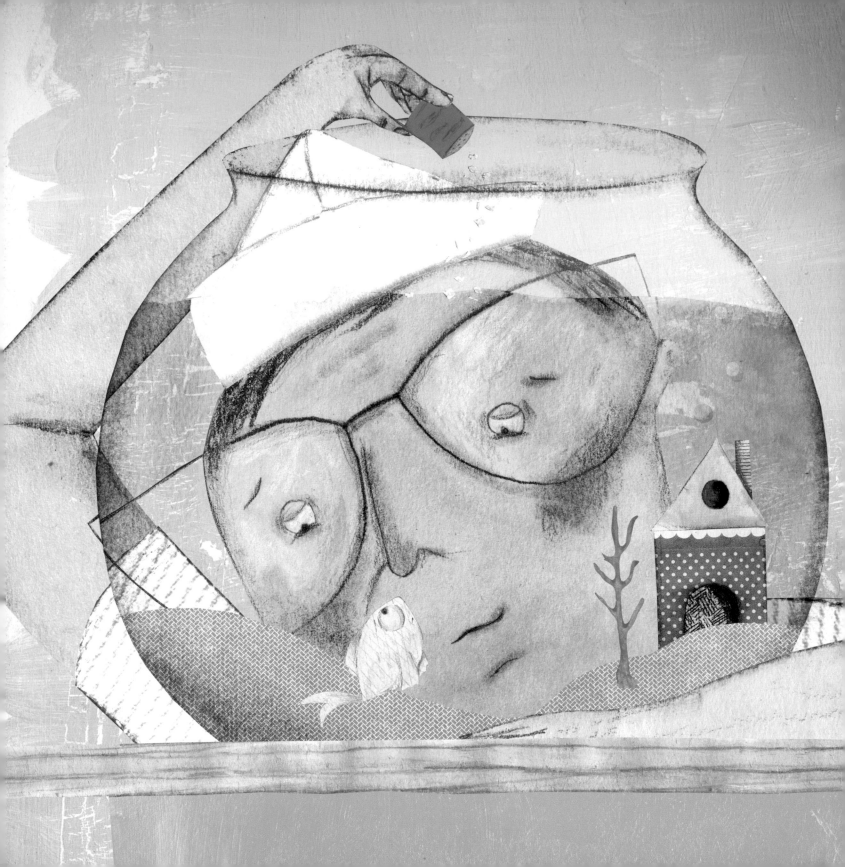

Glub in bowl, all alone, but understanding home. Well-fed,
not dead and still not quite in bed.

"Hey, fish," says Foster with a tired voice. "Can't sleep either?"

"I am Glub." Glub smiles.

Shake, shake, shake. Food falls from the sky.

"I've been working this diner my whole life," whispers Foster,
a reef knot in his throat. "But I wanted to be a sailor when
I was a kid. Did you know that, fish? That was my dream,
to sail the seven seas."

Glub shakes his head. This was news to him.

"You and me, fish, we're kind of alike, huh? People see us
all the time, but they don't know us."

Glub considers. Glub agrees. "We live in a glass house."

Glub in bowl, all alone, with no real home.
Glub swims up. Glub swims down. Right then
left, round and round. Glub sighs.

"What do I *do*?" says Glub, adrift.

"Bubbles!" points Evelyn, laughing.

"Hey, Foster, that fish of yours is a miracle
and a half. This is the happiest I've seen my
baby girl in ages."

"Indeed," considers Glub. "I am Glub,
Maker of Bubbles."

Glub in bowl, all alone, but now with skills to hone. Small bubbles and big bubbles, huge bubbles, too. Long bubbles, short bubbles, yellow, red, blue.

"Hey, fish," says Foster with a yawn, "you sure don't sleep much."

"I am Glub," says Glub. "Maker of Bubbles."

"I can't stop thinking of Jenny. She's a peach. Evelyn, too. Poor thing. I bet she misses her dad. So many lonely people, huh, fish?"

Glub considers. Glub agrees. "And fish," Glub adds.

Glub in bowl, all alone. Confused and concerned.
A question has grown.

"Where do I belong?" wonders Glub, as shadows loom.

"There, see, Ma?" says Sis. "Just like I told you."

"Foster G. Willikers," growls Ma. "A fish in the diner?
Your father would not have approved!"

"Aw, Ma, not you, too," Foster groans.

"No ifs, ands or buts. I'm throwing
that fish out — NOW!"

SPLASH!

A hand crashes from the sky.

Glub swims right.

Glub dekes left.

Glub swims up.

Glub ducks down.

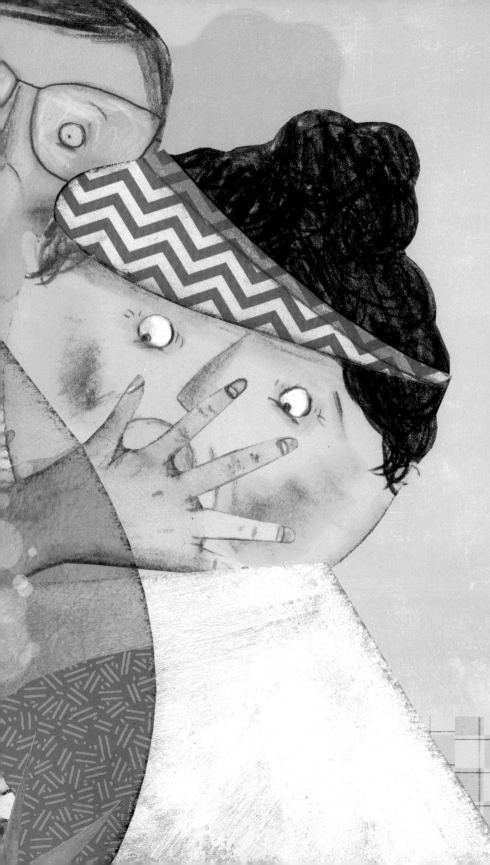

"Have a heart, Mrs. Willikers!" shout the customers. "It's just a fish."

"Just a fish?" asks Glub, electric and humming.

"Hey, look at that! The water is rippling like crazy!"

"Check out all the bubbles!"

"It's a picture!"

"It's a portrait!"

"Why, it's … it's …" trembles Ma, "it's Gerald B. Willikers, my long-departed husband, looking as handsome as ever. How I miss him so. Thank you, fish."

"Wow," thinks Glub. "Did *I* do that?"

Glub in bowl — busy, but still alone.

Fingers touch water, then dreams are shown.

"The fish is right. I have always wanted to be a dancer!"
declares Pete, twirling Sis around.

"It's true. I do miss my old home on the prairies," sighs Doug.

"Outta the way, boys. This gal is going back to school!"
shouts Bernice from atop a chair.

"My turn! My turn!" yell all the others.

"Oh, my, oh, my!" gasps Glub.

Glub in bowl, alone and weary. Full of dreams but not so cheery.

"Hey, fish," mumbles Foster, slumped in a chair. "I guess everyone is happier now because of you."

"I am Glub," sighs Glub. "I make bubbles, just bubbles."

"Oh, well. Maybe happiness is like the flu. Some people catch it and some people don't."

Glub considers. Glub isn't sure.

"Hey, Foster," says Jenny at closing time.

"Aren't you going to have a turn?"

"*Nah*," Foster replies with a shrug.

"Come on," says Jenny. "I'll do it, too."

"Me, me, me!" Evelyn pleads, wanting to be held.

"All of us, on the count of three. One … two …"

"THREE!"

Fish.

Fish *not* in bowl.

"Who am I?" asks fish.

"Glub!" says another, eyes
big and sparkling.

"Glub?" asks fish. "Yes, I *am* Glub!"